This book
belongs to:

_____

MESSAGE TO PARENTS

This book is perfect for parents and children to read aloud together. First read the story to your child. When you read it again, run your finger under each line, stopping at each picture for your child to "read." Help your child to figure out the picture. If your child makes a mistake, be encouraging as you say the right word. Point out the written word beneath each picture in the margin on the page. Soon your child will be "reading" aloud with you, and at the same time learning the symbols that stand for words.

Library of Congress Cataloging-in-Publication Data

Schorsch, Kit.
   The town mouse and the country mouse / retold by Kit Schorsch ; illustrated by Pat Schories.
      p. cm. — (A Read along with me book)
   Summary: A retelling in rebus form of the Aesop fable in which a town mouse and a country mouse exchange visits and discover that each is best suited to his own home.
   ISBN 0-02-898168-5 .
   [1. Fables.   2. Mice—Folklore.   3. Rebuses.] I. Schories, Patricia, ill.   II. Country mouse and the city mouse.   III. Title. IV. Series.
PZ8.2.S36To   1989
398.2'45293233—dc19
[E]   89-692
                                                                              CIP
                                                                              AC

The Town Mouse and the Country Mouse

A Read Along With Me Book

Retold by **Kit Schorsch**
Illustrated by **Pat Schories**

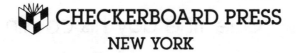

CHECKERBOARD PRESS

NEW YORK

woods

mouse

seeds

nuts

berries

door

Once in the deep there

lived a little country . He led

a very happy life. He always found

plenty to eat. and

and all grew near his front

 .

One fine day his cousin the

town  came to visit.

"Come in! Come in!" said the country . "Please stay for dinner."

"With pleasure," said the town .

The **2** mice sat down at the . The country  put out his best  for his cousin.

The town  looked at the . "You call  and

2 two

table

food

and  dinner?" he said. "You must visit me in my 🏠 in the town. Then you will eat well."

So **3** days later the little country 🐭 locked his 🚪 and set off. Down the winding 🌲 he went to visit his cousin the town 🐭.

When he arrived at the large 🏠 , the country 🐭 was very surprised. It was a wonderful

 . The town 🐭 was waiting

at the front 🚪 .

"Welcome," he said. "The people

have just finished their dinner. Now

we can eat. Follow me."

The town 🐭 led his cousin

through a tiny hole in a 🧱 .

wall

house

mouse

table

food

cheese

"From here we can run through the ," said the town .

They ran and ran. Finally they came out into a room with a large .

The town scampered onto the . His cousin followed.

"Look!" exclaimed the town .

On the was more than the country had ever seen. There was a large ,

sweet  , and  . There was a  and crunchy sugar  . "Now you can taste all the fine  I told you about!" the town  said proudly. But while the 2 mice were eating they heard a noise.

bread

fruit

cake

cookies

two

mouse

maid

table

wall

"Run!" shouted the town 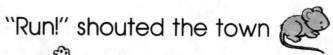.

"The  is coming!" At once

they darted off the 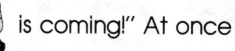 and

hurried into the nearest hole in

the .

The country  was terrified!
In the country he had never run

from anyone.

Hidden behind the , the

town  said, "I always eat after

the people are finished. But I never

know when the 👸 might come.

I have to keep my 👀 and ears

open."

"I like eating in peace," said the

country  .

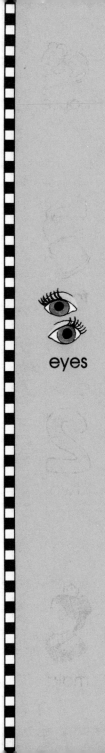

eyes

mouse

food

two

maid

"Don't be silly," said the town . "The danger is worth the taste of real . And anyway, it is safe if you run fast."

The  mice heard the go back to the kitchen. "Come along," said the town  . "It is safe to go back to the  ."

So back the 2 mice scampered to the  . They settled down again to the  , the  , the sugar  , and the  .

But before the 2 mice had eaten very much, they heard a very loud mee-owww.

"Run!" screamed the town  .

table

cheese

bread

cookies

cake

cat

table

wall

mouse

two

"It's the  !" And he quickly

scampered down the leg of the

. Back he ran to the hole in

the . The country

scampered after the town

as fast as he could. And just

behind them came the !

The leaped and pounced

as she tried to catch the

mice.

What a scramble! Into the hole

rushed the town , and after

him tumbled the country .

And not a second too soon. For

the  was thumping and

scratching at the little hole. She

mouse

cat

two

wanted a  for her dinner!

But no matter how much the

scratched and meowed,

the mice were safe.

"Whew!" panted the town

 . "That was a very close call.

You can stop shaking-we are

perfectly safe now."

"Dear me," said the country

 . "I do not like being nearly

eaten while I am eating my dinner.

Not one bit!"

"Your dinner?" said the town

. "What you call in

the country no would eat

in the town. Here we eat REAL

."

"And in the country we have

food

food

food

seeds

nuts

berries

mouse

REAL peace and quiet. Without that

you can't enjoy any kind of

"Peace and quiet and

and  and . No, thank

you. That's not for me," said the

town .

"And this is not for me," said the country . So after quickly looking outside the hole to see if the  was gone, he slipped out. The country  ran happily home along the winding , back to the quiet of the country.

cat

path

Words I can read

- ☐ berries
- ☐ bread
- ☐ cake
- ☐ cat
- ☐ cheese
- ☐ cookies
- ☐ door
- ☐ eyes

- ☐ food
- ☐ fruit
- ☐ house
- ☐ maid
- ☐ mouse
- ☐ nuts
- ☐ path
- ☐ seeds

- ☐ table
- ☐ three
- ☐ two
- ☐ wall
- ☐ woods